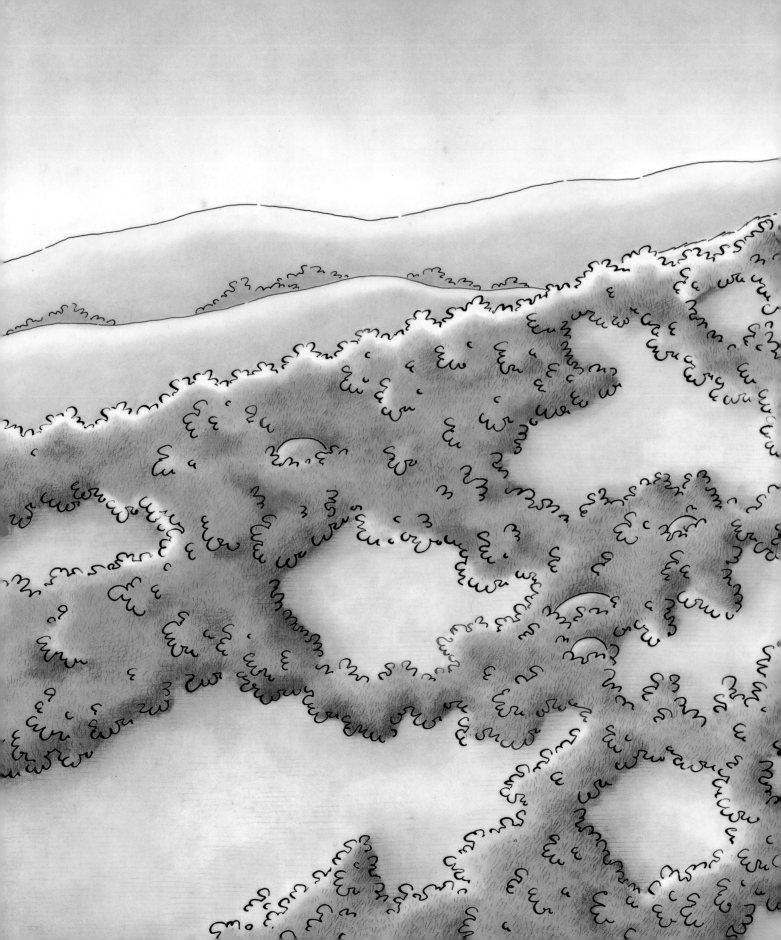

First Aladdin Paperbacks edition 1997. Copyright © 1992 by Lisa Campbell Ernst. Aladdin Paperbacks. An imprint of Simon & Schuster Children's Publishing Division, 1230 Avenue of the Americas, New York, NY 10020. All rights reserved, including the right of reproduction in whole or in part in any form. Also available in a Simon & Schuster Books for Young Readers edition. The text of this book was set in Goudy Old Style. The illustrations were done in pastel, ink, and pencil. Special thanks to Cass. Printed and bound in Hong Kong. 10 9 8 7 6 5 4 3 2 1   The Library of Congress has cataloged the hardcover edition as follows: Ernst, Lisa Campbell. Walter's Tail / by Lisa Campbell Ernst. — 1st American edition.   p.   cm.   Summary: The disasters caused by Walter's wagging tail make him and his owner unwelcome until Walter wags an heroic rescue.   ISBN 0-02-733564-X [1. Dogs—Fiction. 2. Tail—Fiction.] I. Title. PZ7.E7323To 1992[E]—dc20   ISBN 0-689-80963-8 (Aladdin pbk.)

25 Years of Magical Reading

25

ALADDIN PAPERBACKS
EST. 1972

For Spike and Sadie, Cree, Cass,
Yamba, Boomer, and Yogi, who are big—
for Bridget, who will be soon—
and of course for Sally, who will always think she is.

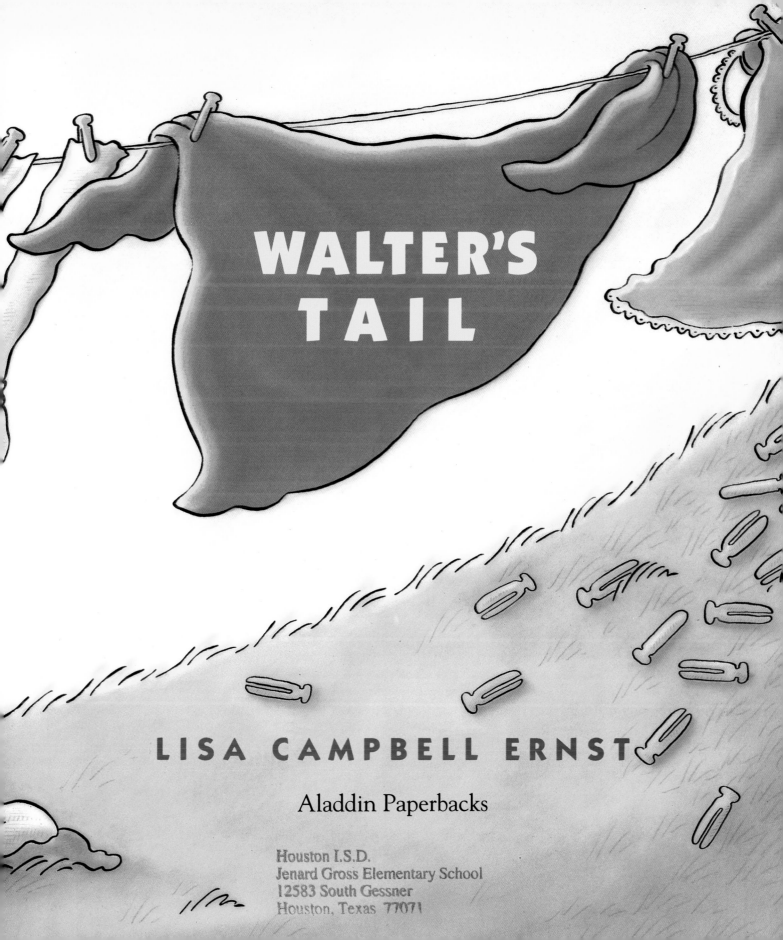

WALTER'S TAIL

LISA CAMPBELL ERNST

Aladdin Paperbacks

Old Mrs. Tully lived in a house on the hill overlooking Walnut Grove. "You shouldn't live up there alone," her town friends insisted.

So Mrs. Tully decided to get a dog.

Mrs. Tully had never had a dog before. But when she saw the puppy whose tail never stopped wagging, it was love at first sight.

"Isn't he cute!" Mrs. Tully declared.

And all of her friends agreed.

"Adorable!" said the grocer.

"Stupendous!" said the florist.

"Magnifique!" said the baker.

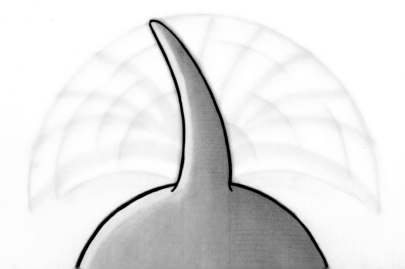

The very happy puppy was named Walter, and Mrs. Tully took him with her everywhere. Each day, friends crowded around to play with precious Walter.

Everyone, of course, was impressed by Walter's most striking feature: his constantly moving tail.

"Does it *ever* stop wagging?" they asked.

"Only when he's asleep," Mrs. Tully said proudly, "and sometimes not even then."

"Isn't that *cute*," they all said.

But then Walter began to grow.
His paws grew. His legs grew. His ears and his nose,
his teeth and his toes, *everything* about Walter grew.
And the one thing that seemed to grow the most
was his ever-moving tail.

That was when the trouble began.

The first accidents happened at home.

Mrs. Tully's favorite vase unexpectedly crashed to the floor as Walter swept past.

Her jigsaw puzzle—the one with 2,768 pieces—somehow shot into the air when Walter turned to leave the room.

And you can imagine what happened when Walter helped Mrs. Tully hang her just-washed dainties out on the clothesline to dry.

Oh, how sorry Walter was after each mishap.

"I didn't mean to," he would say with sad eyes, his tail slowing in regret.

And Mrs. Tully understood. "Don't fret," she'd say, "no harm done, we all make mistakes."

Still, for a while, Walter tried *not* to wag his tail. But it was like trying not to smile when you're happy, or laugh when things are funny. *It just wagged.* There was no stopping it.

Then . . . calamity struck on their daily trip to town.

The grocer was the first to suffer. One whack from Walter's tail sent fancy displays of pears, plums, and pineapples soaring in all directions.

Two weeks later, at the hardware store, nails were spilled, brooms toppled, seeds scattered.

And when Mrs. Tully bought her weekly supply of licorice drops at the candy shop, a barrel of lemon balls tumbled, turning the floor into a lemon-ball sea.

"Oh, we're so very *sorry*," Mrs. Tully cried each time.

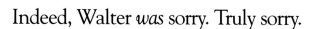

Indeed, Walter *was* sorry. Truly sorry.

But things only got worse. At the florist, flowers lost their petals, pots were smashed to smithereens.

At the beauty shop, Miss Lou's special bottle of Pansy Perfume exploded, like a stink bomb, as it hit the floor.

And the following week at the bakery, the bride and groom atop a fancy wedding cake vanished. Telltale signs of icing were discovered on Walter's wagging tail, but the smiling couple was never found.

By now, Walter and Mrs. Tully's daily visits were the talk of the town. So on the day when Walter truly did "clear the counter" at Belle's Diner, *every*one knew.

Soon people ran the other way when they saw Walter coming. Shopkeepers turned their signs to "closed." Parents shielded their children. And no one ever called Walter's tail "cute" anymore.

"You shouldn't live with such a wild animal!" Mrs. Tully's town friends now told her.

And that is why, after walking down the hill to town for seventy-eight years, Mrs. Tully turned the other way one morning and walked *up* the hill.

"They're right," Mrs. Tully declared. "We're too wild for town. At least we can't cause trouble up here."

So the two set out, with Walter happily sniffing each hillside stone and shrub and flower—wagging, of course, all the way.

Now down below, there was an uneasy silence in town.

At first no one could figure out what was wrong. It was peaceful. . . it was quiet. . . .

Finally someone realized. "It's Mrs. Tully—Mrs. Tully and Walter. Where are they?"

The question buzzed from door to door, from the post office down to the firehouse, from the candy shop to Belle's Diner.

No one had seen Mrs. Tully and Walter.

But from the highest point of the hill, Mrs. Tully and Walter could see *them*. To Walter, the people below looked tiny, like dog toys.

"What a view!" Mrs. Tully shouted. She leaned forward for a better look. "Why there's—"

Suddenly, Mrs. Tully slipped.

As she tumbled backward onto the hard rock, Walter barked in alarm. Worse yet, when Mrs. Tully tried to stand up, she could not pull her foot from a crevice in the rock.

Mrs. Tully was stuck.

Back in town, people were in a real tizzy.

Sure everyone complained about Walter and Mrs. Tully, but being without them felt terrible. Walter and Mrs. Tully were a part of Walnut Grove. They *belonged* there.

Belle from the diner ran up to check Mrs. Tully's house. Empty.

Now everyone began to shout at once.

"Where could they be?"

"What if they're hurt?"

"Where else can we look?"

So noisily were all of Mrs. Tully's friends worrying that they could not hear her faint calls for help, or even Walter's barks, high up on the hill.

Mrs. Tully and Walter watched it all. Pacing back and forth, Walter growled. He felt so helpless.

"Now don't panic," Mrs. Tully said. "Come sit beside me." Walter sat down and Mrs. Tully wrapped her shawl around him. 'We'll think of something," she said, trying to sound cheerful.

And at that very moment, Walter did, indeed, think of something. With a joyful yap he jumped up, pulling the shawl right off of Mrs. Tully's shoulders.

Then, with a dog grin that stretched from ear to ear, Walter began to *do* what Walter did best.

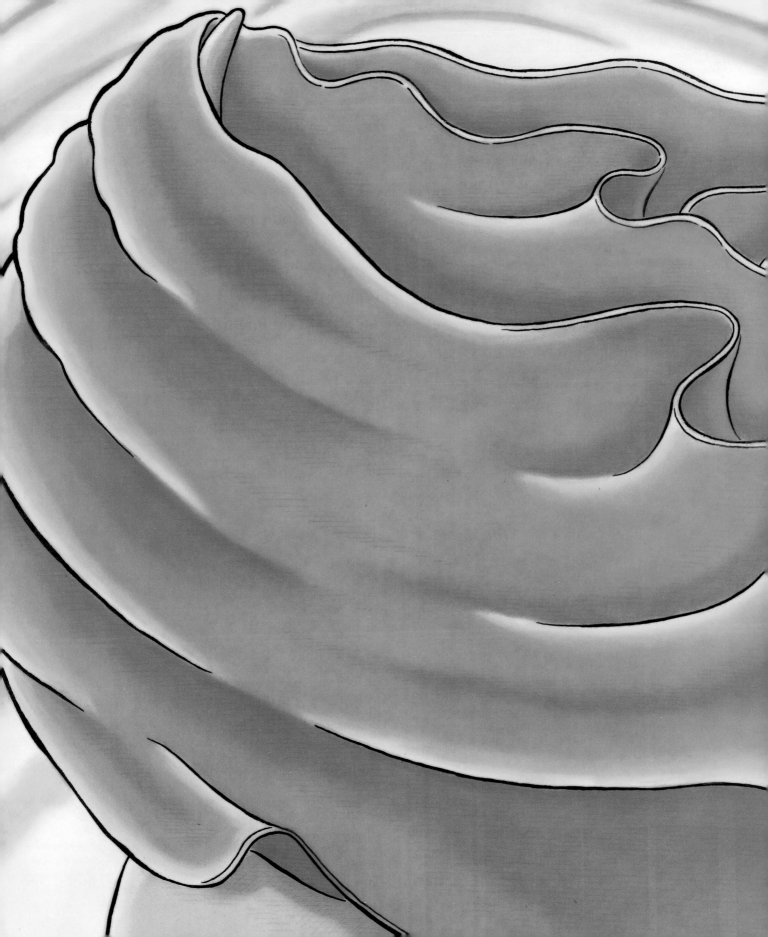

At first the people looking up from town were even more confused. "What—" they stammered. "Who—"

"It's Walter!" someone cried at last. "And he's waving Mrs. Tully's shawl!"

Nearly all of Walnut Grove raced up the hill at once.

The rescue that followed was a joyful hubbub.

Mrs. Tully was safe. And Walter—"The Tail," as he became known—was dubbed a Walnut Grove hero. Naturally, that made Walter's tail wag faster than ever.

"Isn't that *cute*," Mrs. Tully declared every chance she got.

And from that day on, all of her friends were quick to agree.

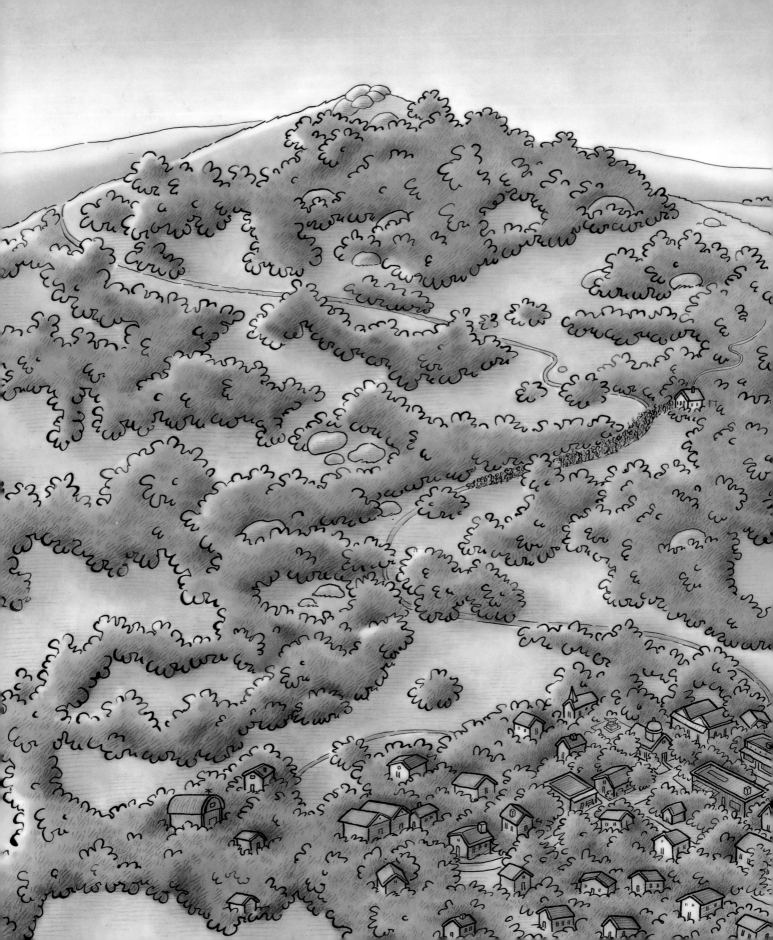

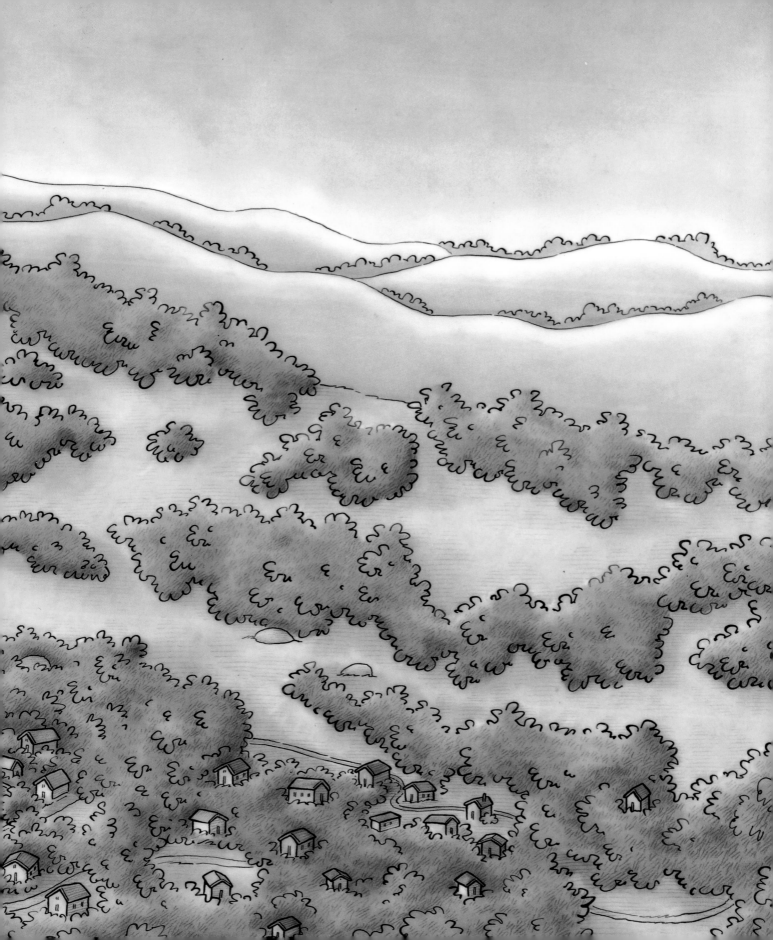